How *Murray* Saved Christmas

Christmas 2004

For Mom and Dad
—M.R.

For Hillary and DJ
—D.C.

PUFFIN BOOKS
Published by Penguin Group
Penguin Young Readers Group,
345 Hudson Street, New York, New York 10014, U.S.A.
Penguin Books Ltd, 80 Strand, London WC2R ORL, England
Penguin Books Australia Ltd, 250 Camberwell Road, Camberwell, Victoria 3124, Australia
Penguin Books Canada Ltd, 10 Alcorn Avenue, Toronto, Ontario, Canada M4V 3B2
Penguin Books (N.Z.) Ltd, 182-190 Wairau Road, Auckland 10, New Zealand

First published in the United States of America by Price Stern Sloan,
a division of Penguin Putnam Books for Young Readers, 2000
Published by Puffin Books, a division of Penguin Young Readers Group, 2004

1 3 5 7 9 10 8 6 4 2

Text copyright © Mike Reiss, 2000
Illustrations copyright © David Catrow, 2000

Set in Bernhart & Bernhart Bold
All rights reserved

LIBRARY OF CONGRESS CATALOGING-IN-PUBLICATION DATA IS AVAILABLE

Puffin Books ISBN 0-14-250145-X

Manufactured in China

How *Murray* Saved Christmas

By Mike Reiss   Illustrated by David Catrow

PUFFIN BOOKS

Twas the night before Christmas and at the North Pole,
Santa was rockin' and ready to roll.
His seat belt was buckled, his reindeer were fed,
And five billion toys were stuffed into his sled.
There were dolls that said "Mama" and dolls that said "goo,"
Dolls that made music and dolls that made poo.
There were dolls that grew tall at the push of a button,
And a doll, best of all, that didn't do nuttin'.

He revved up his reindeer, about to take off,
When all of a sudden he heard a small cough.
"Santa, a-hem, could I have your attention?"
It was Edison Elf with his latest invention.
(Now Edison thought of himself as a tinkerer.
But as a tinkerer, he was sort of a stinkerer.)
"My Jack-in-the-Boxer belongs on your list—
It's a jack-in-the-box with a fabulous twist!"

So Santa Claus tried it,
And, oh, what a trick,
A boxing glove popped out . . .

. . . and knocked out Saint Nick!

He wobbled. He bobbled. His face turned bright red.
A lump like a sugar plum rose from his head!
"SANTA!" cried Eddie. But Santa said, "Glibble.
I'm perfectly shnibble!"—then started to dribble.
Ed dressed him in jammies, and put him to bed.
And worried just who would bring presents instead.
Then a card fluttered down out of Santa's right mitten,
And on it, in round golden letters, was written:
"For special delivery, call Murray Kleiner,
Owner of Murray K's Holiday Diner."

Now Santa and all of the holiday bunch,
Would come into Murray's for breakfast or lunch.
You might see George Washington eatin' and drinkin',
On Presidents' Day with Abraham Lincoln.
Cupid LOVED bagels. The Groundhog . . . the chili.
The Thanksgiving Turkey would stuff himself silly.
And how, you might wonder, did Santa get fat?
Just thank Murray's chocolate-chip cheesecake for that!

But lunchtime was past.
It was late Christmas Eve.
Murray had closed,
And was ready to leave,
When Ed parked the sleigh
And he hollered to Murray,
"I need a delivery
and I'm in a big hurry!"
Murray said, "I can make you
Whatever you wish.
A nice piece of fish.
Or a spinach knish.
But who are you Shorty?
And where is Saint Nick?"
Edison sobbed.
"I made Santa Claus sick!
And now I need you
To deliver some toys . . .
. . . To two hundred countries
. . . To good girls and boys!
Just put on this red suit,
And get in the sleigh."
"What, are you—cuckoo!"
Cried Murray. "No way!"

"Give me one reason to schlep through the snow,
Bringing billions of presents to kids I don't know.
Will anyone pay me? Will anyone tip?
What if I slip and I fracture my hip?
Look out the window—it's cold and it's shivery.
Why in the world should I make this delivery?"

"Because it's Christmas," said Ed.

Christmas, you know, is that one special season,
When people do good things without a good reason.
The grouchiest men will wear musical ties,
And buy Christmas presents for folks they despise.

The cheapest of cheapskates will spend all his money.
And people make fruitcakes from concrete and honey.
Christmas works magic, and Edison knew it.
"You're not playing fair," Murray grumped,
"But I'll do it."

Murray put on the suit—the belly was baggy.
The shoulders were saggy.
The bottom was draggy.
"I'm fat," Murray said, "but it seems Santa's fatter.
The caboose is quite loose, but I guess it won't matter."

Then they hopped in the sleigh, which sped off like a comet,
Causing Murray to holler, "Slow down, or I'll vomit!
I've just got one rule, but, Shorty, it's basic:
If you go too fast then I'm bound to get sleigh-sick!"

They made their first stop, Eddie fearing the worst.
Murray fell down the chimney and landed tush-first.
He didn't come back till a quarter past two.
When Eddie cried, "Murray, what happened to you?"
Murray shrugged. "By the fireplace, kids hung up socks,
So I loaded the socks up with bagels and lox."

They went to the next house—it didn't go better.
Murray got bit by a big Irish setter.
He stepped on a turtle at House Number Three.
At House Number Four, he knocked over the tree.

"I'm old and I'm cold,
and this suit doesn't fit.
If the next stop goes badly,"
Said Murray, "I quit!"
The elf couldn't blame him.
Poor Murray had tried.
"You're going to do great!"
Little Edison lied.
Murray jumped down the chimney,
And landed so hard,
The THUD! knocked the snow
Off the trees in the yard.
He got to his feet,
With an "oof" and an "oy!"
And found himself facing,
A six-year-old boy.

The boy exclaimed, "Santa!" And Murray said, "Where?
Oh, right, you mean me. Yes, I'm Santa, I swear!
Get a load of this laugh—Ho, ho, ho!" Murray chuckled,
But just as he chuckled, his belt came unbuckled,
And his pants, which were loose, went down straight past his knees.
"MURRAY KLEINER" was stitched on his silk BVDs!

The boy looked perplexed, so he said, "Please explain,
Why you and your underpants have different names?"
Betrayed by his boxers. Let down by his pants.
Murray knew a good story would be his best chance.
So he said, "Murray Kleiner's a famous designer.
Calvin Klein may be fine, see, but Kleiner is finer."

"Are you sure you're Santa? You don't have a beard.
Your suit is all baggy. You smell kind of weird."
"I shaved off the beard. Mrs. Claus said it tickles.
. . . And I went on a diet—club soda and pickles.
That should explain why I'm beardless and belly-less.
The pickles would also account for my smelliness.
So there, I've explained. I've made everything clear."
And then the boy asked him to name his reindeer.
Murray hemmed and he hawed—he did not know this stuff,
So he huffed and he puffed and proceeded to bluff:
"There's Dumbo and Jumbo and Mason and Dixon,
Cosmo and Kramer and Richard M. Nixon."
Murray looked at him hopefully, "How did I do?"
"You're a fake!" the boy cried. "I guess Santa is, too."

Murray said, "There's a Santa and I've got the proof!"
They went out on the lawn and looked up at the roof!
"That's Santa's sleigh sitting there in the snow!
There's the toys! And the reindeer whose names I don't know!
Oh, Santa is real, kid. It's wrestling that's fake."
And that's when the boy knew he'd made a mistake . . .
This wasn't just some smelly guy in a suit,
But an honest-to-goodness Saint Nick substitute!

And when the boy smiled, Murray felt a strange tingle,
He knew, for one night, that he could be Kris Kringle!
"HO HO HO!" Murray laughed and he patted his head,
And he fixed him a lean-pastrami sandwich with coleslaw and
a triple-thick chocolate milkshake, and sent him to bed.

Then Edison asked if he still felt like quitting.
"Quitting?" cried Murray. "You've got to be kidding!
Enough of that talk—we've got toys to deliver.
We can't sit around like two lumps of chopped liver!"
From Nome down to Rome, and from Omsk to Atlanta,
They handed out presents more quickly than Santa.

"You did a great job," Eddie said, and he smiled.
"Tonight you brought presents to every good child."
"Let's not stop," Murray said. "We have time. We have toys.
Why can't we bring them to bad girls and boys?
So a kid might be lazy, he might be a slob.
He drives his folks crazy. That's sort of his job!"

Ed heard what he said and he couldn't resist.
They brought toys to the Naughty (a VERY long list!):
A toboggan for Ogden, who played sick from school,
And drove his Dad's Pontiac into the pool.
For Brooke, a good book, since she broke the TV,
The VCR, PC, and every CD.

And a jet plane for Duane (a mischievous fellow!),
Who filled the girls' toilets with blueberry Jell-O.
Murray brought presents to all not-so-good kids.
The rude and the crude and the misunderstood kids.
And people said Christmas was never so pleasant,
As that year when all of the world got a present.

Murray said, "Well, there's nothing for us in this sack."
So he gave Ed a hug, and Ed gave him one back.
"You know, you're a nice guy," said Edison Elf.
"Thanks," Murray said, "you're not half bad yourself.
On, Lipstick! On, Dipstick! On, Pixie and Dixie!
On, Kramden and Norton and Alice and Trixie!"
And Edison said, as they rode out of sight,

"Murray Christmas to all, and to all a good night!"